Asterix Omnibus

ASTERIX THE GLADIATOR, ASTERIX AND THE BANQUET, ASTERIX AND CLEOPATRA

Written by RENÉ GOSCINNY

Illustrated by ALBERT UDERZO

This omnibus © 2008 GOSCINNY/UDERZO

Exclusive licensee: Orion Publishing Group
Translators: Anthea Bell and Derek Hockridge
Typography: Bryony Newhouse

Asterix the Gladiator
Original title: *Astérix Gladiateur*
Original edition © 1964 GOSCINNY/UDERZO
Revised edition and English translation © 2004 HACHETTE

Asterix and the Banquet
Original title: *Le Tour de Gaule d'Astérix*
Original edition © 1965 GOSCINNY/UDERZO
Revised edition and English translation © 2004 HACHETTE

Asterix and Cleopatra
Original title: *Astérix et Cléopâtre*
Original edition © 1965 GOSCINNY/UDERZO
Revised edition and English translation © 2004 HACHETTE

The right of René Goscinny and Albert Uderzo to be identified as the authors of this work
has been asserted by them in accordance with the Copyright, Designs and Patents Act 1988.

This omnibus first published in Great Britain in 2008 by
Orion Books Ltd.
This edition first published in Great Britain in 2011 by Orion Children's Books Ltd.
Orion House
5 Upper St Martin's Lane
London WC2H 9EA
An Hachette Livre UK Company

Printed in China

www.asterix.com/english/
www.orionbooks.co.uk

A CIP catalogue record for this book is available from the British Library

ISBN 978 1 4440 0424 3

The Orion Publishing Group's policy is to use papers that are natural, renewable and recyclable and made
from wood grown in sustainable forests. The logging and manufacturing processes are expected to conform to
the environmental regulations of the country of origin.

Every effort has been made to fulfil requirements with regard to reproducing copyright material.
The author and publisher will be glad to rectify any omissions at the earliest opportunity.

GAULISH VILLAGE

COMPENDIUM

LAUDANUM

AQUARIUM

TOTORUM

ARMORICA

BELGICA

• LUTETIA

SPQR

GAUL
(ROMAN CONQUEST)
50 BC

CELTICA

PROVINCIA

AQUITANIA

THE YEAR IS 50 BC. GAUL IS ENTIRELY OCCUPIED BY THE
ROMANS. WELL, NOT ENTIRELY ... ONE SMALL VILLAGE OF
INDOMITABLE GAULS STILL HOLDS OUT AGAINST THE INVADERS.
AND LIFE IS NOT EASY FOR THE ROMAN LEGIONARIES WHO
GARRISON THE FORTIFIED CAMPS OF TOTORUM, AQUARIUM,
LAUDANUM AND COMPENDIUM ...

ASTERIX, THE HERO OF THESE ADVENTURES. A SHREWD, CUNNING LITTLE WARRIOR, ALL PERILOUS MISSIONS ARE IMMEDIATELY ENTRUSTED TO HIM. ASTERIX GETS HIS SUPERHUMAN STRENGTH FROM THE MAGIC POTION BREWED BY THE DRUID GETAFIX . . .

OBELIX, ASTERIX'S INSEPARABLE FRIEND. A MENHIR DELIVERY MAN BY TRADE, ADDICTED TO WILD BOAR. OBELIX IS ALWAYS READY TO DROP EVERYTHING AND GO OFF ON A NEW ADVENTURE WITH ASTERIX – SO LONG AS THERE'S WILD BOAR TO EAT, AND PLENTY OF FIGHTING. HIS CONSTANT COMPANION IS DOGMATIX, THE ONLY KNOWN CANINE ECOLOGIST, WHO HOWLS WITH DESPAIR WHEN A TREE IS CUT DOWN.

GETAFIX, THE VENERABLE VILLAGE DRUID, GATHERS MISTLETOE AND BREWS MAGIC POTIONS. HIS SPECIALITY IS THE POTION WHICH GIVES THE DRINKER SUPERHUMAN STRENGTH. BUT GETAFIX ALSO HAS OTHER RECIPES UP HIS SLEEVE . . .

CACOFONIX, THE BARD. OPINION IS DIVIDED AS TO HIS MUSICAL GIFTS. CACOFONIX THINKS HE'S A GENIUS. EVERYONE ELSE THINKS HE'S UNSPEAKABLE. BUT SO LONG AS HE DOESN'T SPEAK, LET ALONE SING, EVERYBODY LIKES HIM . . .

FINALLY, VITALSTATISTIX, THE CHIEF OF THE TRIBE. MAJESTIC, BRAVE AND HOT-TEMPERED, THE OLD WARRIOR IS RESPECTED BY HIS MEN AND FEARED BY HIS ENEMIES. VITALSTATISTIX HIMSELF HAS ONLY ONE FEAR, HE IS AFRAID THE SKY MAY FALL ON HIS HEAD TOMORROW. BUT AS HE ALWAYS SAYS, TOMORROW NEVER COMES.

GOSCINNY AND UDERZO
PRESENT
An Asterix Adventure

ASTERIX
THE
GLADIATOR

Written by RENÉ GOSCINNY *and Illustrated by* ALBERT UDERZO

Translated by Anthea Bell *and* Derek Hockridge

THE ROMAN CAMP OF COMPENDIUM IS IN A FERMENT. THE PREFECT OF GAUL, ODIUS ASPARAGUS, IS PAYING A CALL ON CENTURION GRACCHUS ARMISURPLUS. THE PREFECT ARRIVES FROM THE NEARBY COAST WHERE HIS GALLEY HAS PUT IN...

PRESENT... PILUM!...

AVE, PREFECT! THIS IS A GREAT HONOUR FOR ME!

AVE, CENTURION! YOU'RE TELLING ME!

AND NOW FOR THE PURPOSE OF MY VISIT, CENTURION! I'M GOING TO ROME ON LEAVE, AND CUSTOM DECREES THAT I TAKE CAESAR A HANDSOME PRESENT... SOMETHING UNUSUAL AND VERY VALUABLE...

...I DID THINK OF TAKING HIM A PRESENT FROM LUTETIA, MAYBE A MARBLE MEMO TABLET FOR HIM TO CARVE DOWN HIS APPOINTMENTS, BUT THAT'S TOO ORDINARY...

THEN I HAD A BRILLIANT IDEA! WHY NOT TAKE CAESAR ONE OF THE INVINCIBLE GAULS FROM HEREABOUTS?

WHAT?!

BUT, PREFECT, ABOUT THESE INVINCIBLE GAULS... THERE'S JUST ONE SNAG!

WELL, WHAT IS IT?

THEY HAPPEN TO BE INVINCIBLE!

THAT'S WHAT MAKES THEM SO VALUABLE! GET ME ONE OF THESE GAULS, AND YOU WON'T REGRET IT!

THERE'S CERTAINLY ONE WHO'S A BIT MORE HARMLESS THAN THE OTHERS... CACOFONIX THE BARD. HE OFTEN GOES FOR WALKS IN THE FOREST BY HIMSELF LOOKING FOR INSPIRATION!

EXCELLENT! I MUST HAVE THIS BARD – AND FAST!

AND IN THE GAULISH VILLAGE...

GOODBYE, ASTERIX, I'M GOING FOR A WALK IN THE FOREST!

GOODBYE, CACOFONIX!

14

15

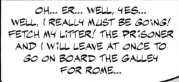

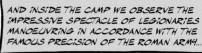

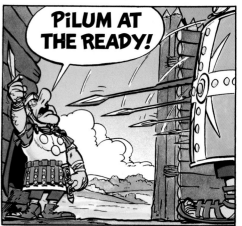

18

SWOOOSH!

I CAN'T FIND CACOFONIX ANYWHERE... AH, THERE'S THE ROMAN COMMANDER!

BANG! BING!

I SHALL FIGHT TO THE DEATH!

WANT ME TO THUMP YOU?

OH ALL RIGHT! ALL IS LOST! I SURRENDER! ALEA JACTA EST!

AND LET IT BE A LESSON TO YOU! NOW, GIVE US BACK OUR BARD, AND DON'T DO IT AGAIN!

THE FACT IS... YOUR BARD ISN'T HERE ANY MORE. AT THIS MOMENT HE'S ON BOARD A GALLEY, SAILING FOR ROME TO BE GIVEN TO CAESAR AS A PRESENT...

!!!

WE'RE WASTING OUR TIME...

A PRESENT? THAT'S A REALLY FUNNY IDEA!

LOOK AT THIS, ASTERIX! I'M SURE I'VE WON OUR BET! AND ONE LEGIONARY WAS FIGHTING BARE-HEADED TOO. IT'S AGAINST ALL THE RULES OF WARFARE TO GO INTO BATTLE IMPROPERLY DRESSED! I'VE A GOOD MIND TO REPORT HIM!

THE GAULS WITHDRAW, LEAVING BEHIND THEM THE AFTERMATH OF BATTLE...

THEY REALLY LET US HAVE IT, EH, SIR?

IN THE FIRST PLACE, GET THIS CAMP BACK INTO ORDER!!! WHAT'S ALL THIS UNTIDINESS IN AID OF? AND DON'T ANYONE EVER MENTION THIS BATTLE TO ME AGAIN!!!

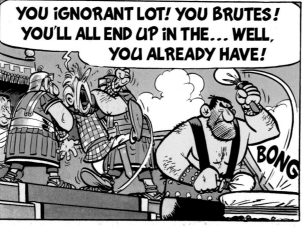

NOW TO STOP THIS SHIP SAILING ALONG THE COAST!

ASTERIX AND OBELIX MAKE THE ANCIENT GAULISH SIGN INDICATING A WISH TO BE TAKEN ON BOARD. NOTE THE FOUR CLENCHED FINGERS AND THE THUMB JERKED IN THE DESIRED DIRECTION. IF YOU WISH TO GO TO ROME, THE DIRECTION OF THE THUMB IS IMMATERIAL, SINCE ALL ROADS LEAD THERE.

N.B. THIS GESTURE IS STILL EMPLOYED TODAY, THOUGH NOT OFTEN TO STOP SHIPS.

IT'S A PHOENICIAN GALLEY. THE PHOENICIANS ARE FAMOUS SAILORS AND MERCHANTS!

WHAT'S THE PHOENICIAN FOR SINGULARIS PORCUS?

WE'RE FROM TYRE IN PHOENICIA. MY NAME IS EKONOMIKRISIS. WOULD YOU LIKE TO BUY ANY GLASS, JEWELS, TEXTILES, PURPLE, FURNITURE?

NO, WE WANT TO GO TO ROME.

HM... ER... ALL RIGHT, COME ON BOARD!

ARE THOSE SLAVES?

OH NO, THEY'RE PARTNERS... WHEN WE FLOATED THE COMPANY, I DREW UP THE CONTRACT AND THEY FAILED TO READ IT CAREFULLY BEFORE SIGNING. I'M CHAIRMAN AND MANAGING DIRECTOR.

IT'S KIND OF YOU TO TAKE US TO ROME. I HOPE IT DOESN'T MEAN GOING OUT OF YOUR WAY?

AS IT HAPPENS, WE WERE PLANNING TO GO TO ROME. ONE OF MY PREDECESSORS ABANDONED HIS SHIP THERE...

IT SANK?

NO, HE SOLD IT. HE WAS A BETTER SALESMAN THAN SAILSMAN.

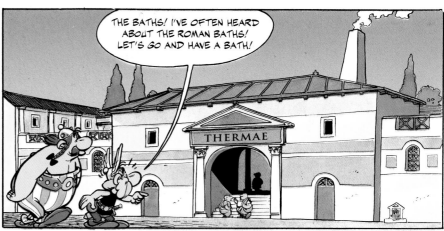

LET'S TRY A FEW CRAFTY QUESTIONS ON THIS GUARD. WE MUSTN'T AROUSE HIS SUSPICIONS...

NO...

HEY, YOU! WHERE'S CACOFONIX IMPRISONED?

?!

CELL XVIIII, FIRST BASEMENT DOWN, BUT IT'S A SECRET!

THERE!

?? ?! ? ? ? ?! ? ? ?

SOON AFTERWARDS...

AND NOW FOR THE CIRCUS. I'LL DRINK A LITTLE MAGIC POTION.

HERE'S MY PLAN – WE KNOCK DOWN EVERYONE AND EVERYTHING UNTIL WE FIND CACOFONIX AND THEN WE MAKE OFF WITH HIM!

THAT'S A CLEVER PLAN!

HALT! NO...

ENTRY!

CELL XV... CELL XVI... CELL XVII... WE'RE GETTING WARM!

OUR BET ABOUT THE HELMETS IS STILL ON, ISN'T IT?

CELL XVIIII IS EMPTY!

HEY! WHAT ARE YOU TWO DOING HERE?

21

33

34

LET'S GET THEM!

SPLAT!

IT'S A NUISANCE, WHAT INSTANTMIX TOLD US...

CLONK!

YES, HEARING THINGS LIKE THAT MAKES ME COME OVER ALL FAINT...

HE SAID ONLY CONDEMNED MEN, LIONS AND GLADIATORS GET INTO THE CIRCUS...

SUPPOSE WE DRESSED UP AS LIONS?

GAULISH RESTAURANT

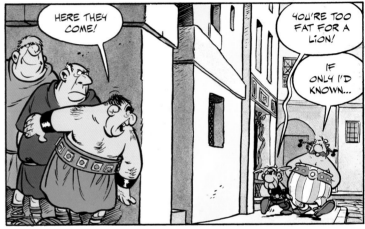

HERE THEY COME!

YOU'RE TOO FAT FOR A LION!

IF ONLY I'D KNOWN...

ALL THE SAME, WE MUST SAVE OUR BARD!

OF COURSE!

LET'S BEAT IT! HERE COME THE COPS!

NOW, NOW, NOW, WHAT'S ALL THIS 'ERE? YOU COME ALONG QUIETLY TO THE STATION! AND NO FUNNY BUSINESS – WE'RE SEVEN TO TWO!

LET'S GET BACK TO OUR INN!

FORWARD, MEN... OUFF!

I SAY, ASTERIX, DON'T YOU THINK IT'S FUNNY, ALL THESE PEOPLE ATTACKING US?

PEOPLE? WHAT PEOPLE?

CIRCUS INN

23

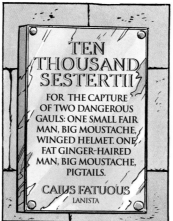

TEN THOUSAND SESTERTII

FOR THE CAPTURE OF TWO DANGEROUS GAULS: ONE SMALL FAIR MAN, BIG MOUSTACHE, WINGED HELMET. ONE FAT GINGER-HAIRED MAN, BIG MOUSTACHE, PIGTAILS.

CAIUS FATUOUS LANISTA

IN THE CIRCUS INN...

OBELIX, I'VE JUST HAD AN IDEA! WE'LL BECOME GLADIATORS!

OH?

AND HOW DO WE GET TO BE GLADIATORS?

WE'LL ASK A ROMAN... THE ONLY ONE WE KNOW IS THAT ONE WHO HAS A LOT OF BATHS. LET'S GO TO THE BATHS!

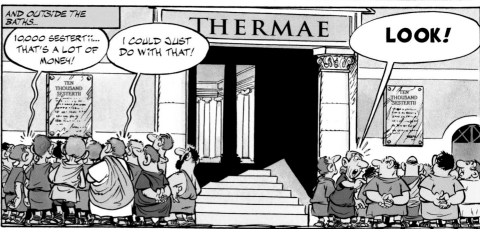

AND OUTSIDE THE BATHS...

10000 SESTERTII... THAT'S A LOT OF MONEY!

I COULD JUST DO WITH THAT!

THERMAE

LOOK!

I SAW THEM FIRST!

NO, ME!

IT'S A LIE! THE 10,000 SESTERTII ARE MINE!

?!???

HERE, LET US BY! WE'RE IN A HURRY.

THESE ROMANS ARE CRAZY!

OH, SO IT'S YOU TWO BACK AGAIN. I THOUGHT I TOLD YOU BEFORE...

OI! TAKE YOUR SANDALS OFF IF YOU WANT TO COME IN THE BATH!

SPLOSH!

24

36

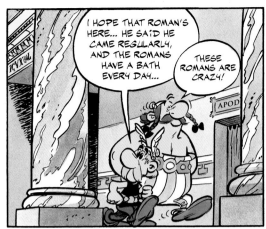

37

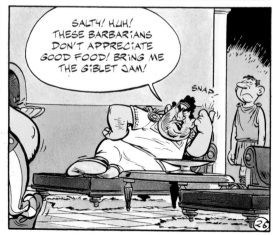

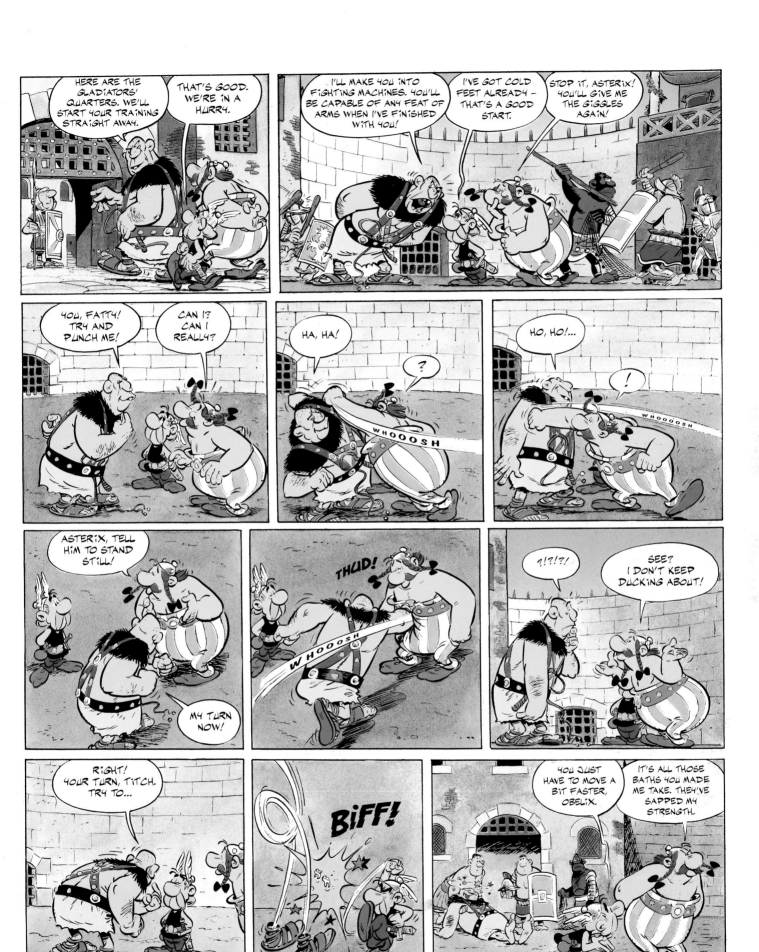

41

GRAND CIRCUS GAMES

IMPRESARIO, CAIUS FATUOUS

CHARIOT RACES

GAULISH BARD
THROWN TO THE LIONS

GLADIATORIAL CONTESTS
WITH
ASTERIX
& OBELIX
THE INDOMITABLE GAULS

(BOOKING OFFICE NOW OPEN)

44

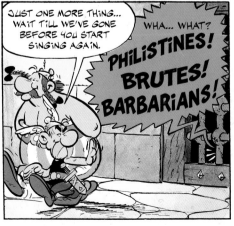

A HUGE CROWD IS FORMING OUTSIDE THE CIRCUS...

WASH YOUR TOGAS IN SUPER PERSIC! SUPER PERSIC WASHES EVEN PURPLER!

SCORE CARD! SCORE CARD!

CUSHIONS! CUSHIONS!

CHIPOLATAE! CANES CALIDI! CHIPOLATAE!

AND INSIDE THE IMPOSING ARENA THE TRUMPETS ANNOUNCE THE ARRIVAL OF CAESAR IN THE IMPERIAL BOX...

TANTAN TARA!!!!

PANEM ET CIRCENSES

LONG LIVE CAESAR!

CAESAR FOR EVER!

EVERYONE APPLAUDS THE DICTATOR...

CLAP! CLAP! CLAP! CLAP! CLAP! CLAP!

CLAP! CLAP! CLAP! CLAP!

CLAP! CLAP!

ET TU BRUTE!*

CLAP! CLAP! CLAP!

CLAP! CLAP! CLAP! CLAP! CLAP!

* YOU TOO, BRUTUS!

THAT BRUTUS... I CAN SEE I'M GOING TO HAVE TROUBLE WITH HIM.*

CLAP! CLAP! CLAP! CLAP! CLAP! CLAP! CLAP! CLAP!

* AN EXAMINATION OF ACT III, SCENE 1 OF JULIUS CAESAR BY WILLIAM SHAKESPEARE WILL INDICATE THE PROPHETIC NATURE OF THIS REMARK.

THIS WILL BE A GREAT SHOW, O CAESAR!

I HOPE SO, CAIUS FATUOUS. IF NOT, YOU'LL BE IN ON THE ACT.

LET THE GAMES BEGIN!

GULP!

34

48

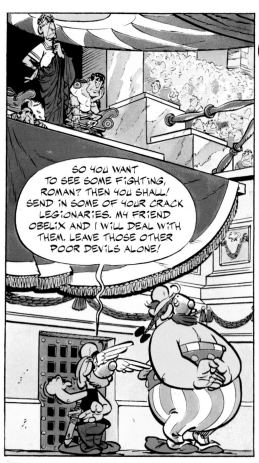

...AND FINALLY I ASK YOU TO FREE THE GLADIATORS. THEY'RE GIVING UP THEIR BLOODTHIRSTY JOB!

GRANTED, O GAUL!

MMPH? IS THE SHOW OVER YET?

I ASK YOU TO FREE THE BARD WE CAME TO RESCUE, AND LET US GO HOME TO GAUL BEFORE WE HAVE TO BEAT YOUR ARMY UP AGAIN...

AND I HAVE ONE LAST FAVOUR TO ASK YOU, JULIUS...

YOU SAW THAT? NOT A BAD PROGRAMME, EH?

LEND US CAIUS FATUOUS THE GLADIATOR TRAINER FOR OUR JOURNEY BACK TO GAUL. WE'LL SEND HIM BACK BY RETURN.

GRANTED, BY JUPITER!

BUT... BUT...

WHAT ARE YOU GOING TO DO WITH ME?

WE'RE GOING TO TEACH YOU A LITTLE LESSON, BY BELENOS!

LONG LIVE THE GAULS!

LONG LIVE THE GLADIATORS!

LONG LIVE CAESAR!

WHAT HAPPENED TO ME?

EXACTLY WHAT WILL HAPPEN AGAIN IF YOU DARE SING A NOTE BEFORE WE GET BACK TO GAUL!

NO FEAR! I'M NOT SINGING FOR ANY MORE ROMAN BARBARIANS, AND MOREOVER I'M TAKING NO FURTHER INTEREST IN THE MATTER!

HEY, WHERE ARE THE RUINS? DIDN'T A HOUSE FALL ON ME?

42

AND AFTER A FEW HOURS' WALK...

O EKONOMIKRISIS, PHOENICIAN MERCHANT, WILL YOU KEEP YOUR PROMISE AND TAKE US BACK TO GAUL?

MY OLD FRIENDS THE GAULS!!!

COME ABOARD, FRIENDS! BUSINESS WAS GOOD. I HAVE SOLD EVERYTHING, AND NOW I HAVE TO STOCK UP AGAIN!

WHO'S THIS?

A LITTLE SURPRISE FOR YOUR ROWING PARTNERS!

DO I ... DO I HAVE TO ROW ALL BY MYSELF? ALL THE WAY BACK TO GAUL?

THIS WILL TEACH YOU TO DO A DIRTY JOB AND LIVE OFF OTHER PEOPLE'S MUSCLE!

WHY DON'T I SING A LITTLE SOMETHING TO LIVEN HIM UP?

NOOOO!

HE'S GREAT!

WHAT AN OARSMAN!

HEAR, HEAR!

SPLAT! SPLAT! SPLAT! SPLAT! SPLAT! SPLAT!

I FEEL WE MIGHT MAKE THIS ROMAN A PARTNER!

AN EXCELLENT NOTION, MR. CHAIRMAN!

BAH!

THE VOYAGE IS UNEVENTFUL, EXCEPT FOR A SKIRMISH WITH THE PIRATES...

CHEER UP, CAP'N! WE'RE ALL IN THE SAME BOAT!

43

55

THE END

56

GOSCINNY AND UDERZO
PRESENT
An Asterix Adventure

ASTERIX AND THE BANQUET

Written by RENÉ GOSCINNY *and Illustrated by* ALBERT UDERZO

Translated by Anthea Bell *and* Derek Hockridge

PEACE REIGNS IN THE FORTIFIED ROMAN CAMP OF COMPENDIUM...

?!

♪♫♪

ZZZZ

UNTIL...

O CENTURION LOTUSEATUS, THERE'S A VISITOR FROM ROME FOR YOU. LOOKS LIKE TOP BRASS!

HE DOES?

AVE! I AM INSPECTOR GENERAL OVERANXIUS, WITH THE RANK OF PREFECT, ON A SPECIAL MISSION FROM JULIUS CAESAR!

AVE.

ER... PLEASED TO MEET YOU... AND HOW'S CAESAR?

FED TO THE TEETH, BY JUPITER! THAT'S WHY I'M HERE! ALL GAUL IS AT PEACE WITH THE LIBERATING ROMAN ARMY, EXCEPT THIS ONE LITTLE VILLAGE OF DISSIDENTS HERE IN YOUR SECTOR DEFYING THE POWER OF CAESAR!

S... SO?

SO I AM GOING TO LEAD YOUR MEN AGAINST THE VILLAGERS. I'LL SOON GET THEM INTO LINE!

BUT... BUT THOSE GAULS ARE DANGEROUS! THEY HAVE MAGICAL POWERS...

NONSENSE! SOUND THE ASSEMBLY!

WE'RE ENTERING THE LISTS! HOLD THE GAULS AT BAY, AND IT WILL BE ANOTHER BAYLEAF IN CAESAR'S WREATH!*

THE GAULS?!

*WE WOULD SAY: ANOTHER FEATHER IN HIS CAP.

DIRECTLY AFTERWARDS...

I DIDN'T MEAN THE SICK BAY! WHERE'S YOUR PILUM?

SICK BAY

IT MAY BE A BITTER PILUM, BUT WE PREFER THE SICK LISTS.

AND A SHORT, SHARP BATTLE BETWEEN GAULS AND ROMANS ENSUES...

TCHAC!
PAF!
PIF!
BY JUPITER!
CHTIAFF!
BY TOUTATIS!
BYE-BYE!
BING!
TCHRAAC!

I TELL YOU THIS ONE'S MINE, FULLIAUTOMATIX!

OH NO, IT ISN'T! OH NO, IT ISN'T! YOU'VE HAD FOUR ALREADY. I'VE BEEN COUNTING!

YOU CAN STOP ARGUING, THEY'RE OFF.

?!?

NO! NO! COME BACK! OH, PLEASE COME BACK!

IF WE'VE QUITE FINISHED, MAY I LEAVE THE BATTLEFIELD?

AND BACK IN COMPENDIUM...

SICK BAY

I ASK YOU! WAS IT WORTH BEING THUMPED JUST TO LAND UP BACK HERE?

I DID WARN YOU, OVERANXIUS!

GNGNGNGNGNGN GNGNGNGNGN!

WELL, IF THAT'S HOW IT IS, I HAVE ANOTHER IDEA! WE SHALL ISOLATE THE GAULISH VILLAGE FROM THE OUTSIDE WORLD!

SOON AFTERWARDS...

EXEGI MONUMENTUM AERE PERENNIUS.

LET'S HOPE YOU'RE RIGHT!

O CHIEF VITALSTATISTIX, THE ROMANS ARE PUTTING UP A STOCKADE ALL ROUND THE VILLAGE!

GOODNESS ME, WHAT FOR? LET'S TAKE A LOOK...

THESE ROMANS ARE CRAZY!

SINCE YOU'RE SO CLEVER, BY MINERVA, I'M SHUTTING YOU UP IN YOUR VILLAGE! YOU WON'T BE ABLE TO GO SPREADING YOUR SEDITIOUS OPINIONS THROUGH GAUL!

YOU'LL HAVE TO BE SELF-SUFFICIENT AND LIVE ON THE PRODUCE OF YOUR OWN VILLAGE! THE OUTSIDE WORLD WILL FORGET YOU!

GAUL IS OUR COUNTRY, O ROMAN, AND WE'LL GO WHERE WE LIKE IN IT...

I'LL MAKE A BET WITH YOU: WE SHALL GET OUT OF OUR VILLAGE IN SPITE OF YOUR STOCKADE AND YOUR LEGIONARIES, AND WE'LL GO ON A TOUR OF GAUL...

...BRINGING BACK ALL ITS REGIONAL SPECIALITIES! ON OUR RETURN, WE'LL INVITE YOU TO A BANQUET TO PROVE WE ARE TELLING THE TRUTH!

HARGH HARGH GNGNGNGN!!

DONE, O GAULS! IF YOU WIN YOUR BET I WILL RAISE THE SIEGE AND GO BACK TO ROME TO TELL JULIUS CAESAR I'VE FAILED!

AND WHEN YOU GET THERE, GIVE OUR REGARDS TO OUR OLD FRIEND CAIUS FATUOUS.

KEEP AN EYE ON THEM!

AN EYE IT'LL HAVE TO BE... I CAN'T OPEN THE OTHER ONE YET!

WHILE THE GAULS WERE ATTACKING US TO THE SOUTH, SOME OF THEM GOT OUT HERE AFTER THUMPING THE SENTRY.

IF ONLY WE KNEW WHICH ONES!

JOIN THE ARMY, THEY SAID. IT'S A MAN'S LIFE, THEY SAID...

OH, THAT'S EASY! IT'LL HAVE BEEN ASTERIX AND OBELIX. THAT PAIR ARE ALWAYS TRYING TO MAKE US LOOK SILLY... AND REMEMBER, IT WAS ASTERIX WHO MADE THAT BET WITH YOU!

WELL, THEY WON'T GET FAR! I WANT THE ENTIRE ARMY OF OCCUPATION ALERTED ALL OVER GAUL! SEND A DESPATCH RIDER OFF AT ONCE!

WE'LL BE THE LAUGHING-STOCK OF GAUL IF THEY WIN THAT BET!

MEANWHILE...

WE MAY HAVE TIME TO REACH ROTOMAGUS* BEFORE THEY RAISE THE ALARM.

* ROUEN

AND FROM ROTOMAGUS WE CAN GO ALONG THE RIVER TO LUTETIA, OUR FIRST STOPPING PLACE.

LOOK, ASTERIX! THERE'S A ROMAN SOLDIER ON HORSEBACK.

AFTER A LONG WALK...

O NORMAN FULFILLING YOUR NORM, IS THIS THE WAY TO ROTOMAGUS?

COULD BE. COULDN'T SAY FOR SURE.

I THOUGHT IT WAS A BUCKET HE WAS FILLING. IS IT FAR?

COULD BE NOT. COULDN'T SAY FOR SURE.

THIS COULD BE IT, OBELIX, BUT I COULDN'T SAY FOR SURE...

ROTOMAGVS

66

YOU CAN STOP NOW, OBELIX. WE'VE GOT TO LUTETIA.

NOT TOO TIRED?

OH NO. CRUISING DOWN THE RIVER IS VERY RESTFUL.

THERE'S NOTHING TO WORRY ABOUT IN LUTETIA. THE ROMANS WILL NEVER FIND US IN THE CROWD.

HELLO, THEY HAVEN'T SORTED IT OUT SINCE WE WERE LAST HERE.*

GET A MOVE ON!

YOU HEARD HIM! MOVE!

SO JUST WHERE DO I MOVE, GRANDPA?

I'VE BEEN HERE TWO DAYS NOW!

HEAR THAT? SOMEONE NEW!

* SEE ASTERIX AND THE GOLDEN SICKLE

THESE MINIS CAN NIP IN ANYWHERE!

WE'RE GOING TO BUY SOME HAM. LUTETIA IS FAMOUS FOR ITS HAM!

PORK BUTCHER

YES, A WHOLE HAM, AND DON'T SLICE IT TOO THIN...

GET YOUR CART OUT OF THE WAY! YOU'RE BLOCKING THE ROAD!

SO WHAT? I'M UNLOADING, AREN'T I?

WELL, HERE COMES A PATROL! WE'LL SEE WHAT THEY SAY ABOUT IT!

A PATROL! LET'S GET OUT!

69

75

77

HERE WE ARE... A GARRISON TOWN, HE SAID...

DIVODURUM

ASTERIX MUST HAVE BEEN TAKEN TO PRISON. NOW THE BEST WAY TO FIND THE PRISON AND GET INSIDE WOULD BE TO GET TAKEN TO PRISON MYSELF...

SO AS SOON AS I SEE A LEGIONARY I'LL SLAP HIS FACE AND HE'LL CART ME OFF TO PRISON... AH, HERE COMES A GOOD ONE!

PAF!

WELL, COME ON, THEN! PUT ME IN IRONS, CAN'T YOU? TAKE ME TO PRISON!

HEY, TAKE ME TO PRISON! I'VE KNOCKED OUT A LEGIONARY!

QUICK, LEAVE THE LEGIONARY THERE AND HIDE, OR THE ROMANS WILL TAKE YOU PRISONER!

BUT I WANT THEM TO TAKE ME PRISONER! I'M LOOKING FOR THE PRISON!

YOU ARE? WELL, IF YOU'RE SURE YOU WANT THE PRISON, TAKE THE THIRD TURNING ON THE RIGHT.

THANKS.

THIS IS YOURS. I KNOCKED HIM OUT. CAN I COME IN?

?!??

OBELIX!

ASTERIX! AT LAST! I'VE HAD TROUBLE FINDING YOU. COME ON, LET'S GO.

18V

78

79

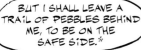

LET'S GO IN FOR A BITE AND A SUP AND A LITTLE INFORMATION.

HEY, CÉSAR! COMPANY!

CAESAR?!

NO, NOT THAT ONE! I'M NOT JULIUS CAESAR, I'M CÉSAR DRINKLIKAFIX, LANDLORD OF THIS INN.

PLEASED TO MEET YOU... CAN YOU TELL US WHERE WE CAN BUY SOME FISH STEW TO TAKE AWAY?

FISH STEW?

HEY, HYDROPHOBIA! GET SOME FISH STEW COOKING!

HAVE A PASTIX?

NO THANKS, WE'D RATHER HAVE GOAT'S MILK...

AND A BOAR, IF YOU'VE GOT ONE...

GOAT'S MILK... BOAR... YOU WOULDN'T BE THE TWO GAULS THOSE CRAZY ROMANS ARE AFTER, WOULD YOU?

THAT'S US.

THEN WELCOME TO MASSILIA! DRINKS ALL ROUND ON ME! MILK FOR YOU, PASTIX FOR US!

NOT FOR ME, THANKS...

WHEN I OFFER DRINKS ON THE HOUSE, SIR, PEOPLE DRINK THEM, IF THEY DON'T WANT TO SEEM LIKE A FISH OUT OF WATER!

90

91

ALL OVER GAUL, THE INFURIATED ROMANS ARE PUTTING UP POSTERS OFFERING A REWARD FOR THE CAPTURE OF OUR FRIENDS...

50,000 SESTERTII REWARD FOR INFORMATION LEADING TO THE ARREST OF

ASTERIX & OBELIX THE TWO DANGEROUS OUTLAWS

AND IN THE TOWN OF AGINUM*...

GOOD FOR THEM!

YOU COULDN'T CALL THEM HANDSOME, BUT THEY HAVE CHARISMA!

I WONDER IF THEY'LL BE STOPPING HERE ON THEIR TOUR OF GAUL?

I'M SURE THEY WILL. THEY'LL WANT TO BUY OUR FAMOUS PRUNES. I HEARD THEY'VE BEEN SEEN IN TOLOSA!

50,000 SESTERTII REWARD FOR INFORMATION LEADING TO THE ARREST OF
ASTERIX & OBELIX THE TWO DANGEROUS OUTLAWS

* AGEN

IN THE ROMAN GARRISON COMMANDER'S OFFICE...

THESE TWO GAULS ARE VERY STRONG. I'VE THOUGHT OF A CUNNING STRATAGEM...

I'LL GIVE THEM DRUGGED FOOD TO EAT, THEY WILL FALL ASLEEP, AND ALL YOU HAVE TO DO IS PICK THEM UP FROM MY INN.

NOT THE KIND OF THING I REALLY LIKE, BUT ALL RIGHT, UPTOTRIX.

NOT A MOMENT TO LOSE! I MUST GO AND MEET THEM!

THEY'RE COMING! THEY'RE COMING!

ASTERIX AND OBELIX'S TOUR OF GAUL IS MORE LIKE A ROMAN TRIUMPH...

THREE CHEERS!

VERY NICE OF THEM, BUT THE ROMANS MIGHT NOTICE SOMETHING...

KEEP GOING!

WAIT A MINUTE, FRIENDS! YOU ARE NATIONAL HEROES... WOULD YOU DO ME THE HONOUR OF TAKING REFRESHMENT AT MY HUMBLE INN?

?!?

MY NAME IS UPTOTRIX. I CAN OFFER YOU PRUNES AND WILD BOAR!

LET'S BE CAREFUL, OBELIX. WE'VE ALREADY BEEN BETRAYED ONCE.

BOAR! OH, COME ON ASTERIX!

NEWS OF THE SENSATIONAL CAPTURE HAS REACHED THE TOWN OF BURDIGALA*...

WHAT A SHAME!

OUR POOR FELLOW-COUNTRYMEN!

TO FAIL AT THIS STAGE!

IF ONLY WE COULD HELP THEM!

* BORDEAUX

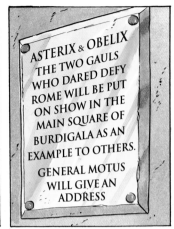

ASTERIX & OBELIX THE TWO GAULS WHO DARED DEFY ROME WILL BE PUT ON SHOW IN THE MAIN SQUARE OF BURDIGALA AS AN EXAMPLE TO OTHERS.

GENERAL MOTUS WILL GIVE AN ADDRESS

...AND THIS BAG OF FOOD, DESTINED FOR THE GAULISH BANQUET, IS PROOF POSITIVE THAT THESE TWO NOTORIOUS OUTLAWS, WHO DARED DEFY THE MIGHT OF ROME, HAVE FAILED IN THEIR ATTEMPT!

BUT I TELL YOU WE'RE VILLANUS...

...AND UNSCRUPULUS!

THEY'RE TELLING THE TRUTH!

?!

AND WE'D LIKE OUR SHOPPING BAG BACK. WE'RE IN A HURRY.

ASTERIX AND OBELIX! THREE CHEERS!

COME ON, LADS, HELP THEM!

OUR HEROES!

LEGIONARIES! SEIZE THOSE MEN!

97

98

101

102

AND THAT EVENING OVERANXIUS COMES GNASHING HIS TEETH, TO SINK THEM IN THE EVIDENCE...

HERE ARE THE THINGS TO EAT AND DRINK WE'VE BROUGHT BACK FROM ALL OVER GAUL... HAM FROM LUTETIA, HUMBUGS FROM CAMARACUM, DUROCORTORUM WINE...

...SAUSAGE FROM TOLOSA, SAUSAGE FROM LUGDUNUM, SALAD FROM NICAE, FISH STEW FROM MASSILIA, OYSTERS AND WINE FROM BURDIGALA.

BUT THERE'S STILL ONE COURSE MISSING... THE SPECIALITY OF THIS VILLAGE!

QUITE RIGHT, OBELIX!

WOOF! WOOF!

?!

O OVERANXIUS, YOU KNOW WHICH CUT OF MEAT IS OUR OWN SPECIALITY?

?

THE UPPERCUT!

TCHAC!

AND OUR FRIENDS HOLD A MAGNIFICENT BANQUET TO CELEBRATE THEIR TRIUMPHANT TOUR OF GAUL, PUTTING BACK ALL THE DELICIOUS FOOD AND WINE OF THEIR BEAUTIFUL AND BELOVED COUNTRY... AS INSPECTOR GENERAL OVERANXIUS COULD CONFIRM, IT IS A GENUINE THREE-STAR MEAL...

44

THE END

GOSCINNY AND UDERZO
PRESENT
An Asterix Adventure

ASTERIX
AND
CLEOPATRA

Written by RENÉ GOSCINNY *and Illustrated by* ALBERT UDERZO

Translated by Anthea Bell *and* Derek Hockridge

ALEXANDRIA, CAPITAL OF EGYPT. THE PALACE OF THE FABULOUS QUEEN CLEOPATRA, OF WHOM IT WAS SAID THAT IF HER NOSE HAD BEEN SHORTER IT WOULD HAVE CHANGED THE WHOLE COURSE OF HISTORY...

THAT'S AN INFAMOUS SUGGESTION, O CAESAR!

YOU HAVE TO FACE FACTS, O QUEEN! YOURS IS A DECADENT NATION, ONLY FIT TO LIVE IN SEMI-SLAVERY UNDER THE ROMANS.

MY PEOPLE BUILT THE PYRAMIDS! THE TOWER OF PHAROS! THE TEMPLES – THE OBELISKS!

THAT'S OLD HAT! ALL THEY CAN DO NOW IS WAIT FOR THE ANNUAL FLOODING OF THE NILE!

THAT WILL DO!

CRASH!

I, CLEOPATRA, WILL PROVE TO YOU, O CAESAR, THAT MY PEOPLE ARE AS BRILLIANT AS EVER! IN THREE MONTHS' TIME I'LL HAVE A MAGNIFICENT PALACE BUILT HERE FOR YOU IN ALEXANDRIA!

WELL, IF YOU CAN DO THAT, O QUEEN, I'LL ADMIT THAT THE EGYPTIANS ARE STILL A GREAT NATION...

...BUT I HAVE MY DOUBTS!

SHE'S A NICE GIRL, ONLY HER NOSE IS SO EASILY PUT OUT OF JOINT...

CRASH!

...PRETTY NOSE TOO!

SOON AFTER-WARDS...

N.B FOR THE CONVENIENCE OF OUR READERS, WE GIVE A DUBBED VERSION OF THE ORIGINAL DIALOGUE...

EDIFIS, I HAVE SUMMONED YOU BECAUSE YOU ARE THE BEST ARCHITECT IN ALEXANDRIA ...WHICH ISN'T SAYING MUCH.

OH!*

* OWING TO THE FACT THAT DUBBING TECHNIQUES HAD NOT BEEN PERFECTED AT THIS PERIOD, THE MOVEMENT OF THE LIPS DOES NOT SYNCHRONIZE VERY WELL WITH THE WORDS.

DON'T ANSWER BACK! YOUR BUILDINGS ARE FLIMSY! YOU CAN HEAR EVERY WORD THE NEIGHBOURS SAY! THE CEILINGS FALL IN!

IT'S THESE MODERN MATERIALS... ACTUALLY, WHAT I REALLY WANT TO DO IS BUILD PYRAMIDS AND...

SILENCE! YOU HAVE JUST THREE MONTHS TO MAKE GOOD. YOU ARE TO BUILD JULIUS CAESAR A MAGNIFICENT PALACE HERE IN ALEXANDRIA.

DID YOU SAY **THREE MONTHS**?

IF YOU SUCCEED I WILL COVER YOU WITH GOLD! IF NOT, YOU'LL BE THROWN TO THE CROCODILES! YOU MAY GO!

THREE MONTHS! I'D NEED SUPERNATURAL POWERS TO DO THAT! I'D NEED SOMEONE WHO CAN WORK MAGIC...

GOT IT! I KNOW THE VERY MAN! HE CAN WORK MAGIC!

CLAC!

AND FAR AWAY, IN A LITTLE VILLAGE IN GAUL...

VI. VI. VI* AGAIN, IT'S LIKE MAGIC!

HA! HA! IT **IS** MAGIC!

THIS ROMAN GAME WILL NEVER CATCH ON...

* 3 SIXES

110

MY SHIP IS WAITING OFFSHORE.

JUST GIVE US TIME TO PACK AND SAY GOODBYE, AND WE'LL BE WITH YOU!

COME ALONG, DOGMATIX, WE'RE GOING ON A NICE SEA VOYAGE!

YOU'RE NEVER GOING TO TAKE HIM?

AND WHY NOT, MAY I ASK, MR ASTERIX?

BECAUSE HE'S TOO SMALL FOR SUCH A LONG JOURNEY, THAT'S WHY NOT, MR OBELIX!

WHAT'S MORE, THERE ARE CATS IN EGYPT! NO, NOT ANOTHER WORD! YOU GO AND PACK.

IT'S ALWAYS THE SAME! I'M JUST AN EXTRA! A MAKEWEIGHT! NO ONE EVER LISTENS TO ME!

SOON AFTERWARDS

YOU, MY FRIENDS, ARE TO REPRESENT THE SPIRIT OF GAUL ON THE BANKS OF THE NILE! SHOW YOURSELVES TRUE-BORN GAULS, BY TOUTATIS, AND MAY THE SKY NEVER FALL ON YOUR HEADS!

HEY!

GOODBYE, THEN, AND THANKS, CHIEF VITALSTATISTIX!

HEY!

EH?

NO, CACOFONIX, YOU ARE NOT, REPEAT NOT, GOING TO SING !!!

BOING! BOING! BOING!

BUT I WASN'T GOING TO SING! I ONLY WANTED TO TELL HIM HE WAS TREADING ON MY TOE!

SOON AFTERWARDS...

WOOF!

?

JUST ME BARKING! I CAN BARK, CAN'T I, EVEN IF I'M NOT ALLOWED TO TALK?

ALL RIGHT, YOU WIN, YOU PIGHEADED GREAT IDIOT! LET HIM OUT!

THERE'S MY SHIP, THE NASTIUPSET.

WE CAN CAST OFF NOW, SETHISBACKUP?

HONESTLY, ASTERIX, I SWEAR I DON'T KNOW HOW HE GOT INTO MY BAG!

NO, NO, OF COURSE NOT! HURRY UP OR WE'LL MISS THE TIDE.

AND WITH AN ICY WINTER WIND BEHIND THEM, OUR FRIENDS SET SAIL ON THEIR LONG VOYAGE TO EGYPT AND THE FABULOUS CLEOPATRA...

IN EGYPT WE SHALL HAVE TO CONTEND WITH LABOUR TROUBLES, THE TIME FACTOR, THE ROMANS, WHO WON'T WANT US TO WIN CLEOPATRA'S BET...

AND ABOVE ALL WITH ARTIFIS, A RIVAL ARCHITECT. HE'S ALWAYS GOT IT IN FOR ME. HE HAS A LOT OF TALENTS...

CLEVER, IS HE?

NO, RICH. HE HAS A LOT OF GOLD TALENTS – THAT'S THE MONEY WE USE IN EGYPT.

AND THEN THERE'S ALWAYS THE DANGER OF PIRATES ON THE WAY.

OH, WE'LL TAKE CARE OF THAT! RIGHT, OBELIX?

SURE ENOUGH, NOT FAR AWAY...

RIGHT, BOYS! WE'RE STEERING CLEAR OF ALL GAULS THIS TIME! AVOID ROMAN AND PHOENICIAN VESSELS TOO – THEY SOMETIMES USE THOSE. I'M PLAYING SAFE... I HAD TO LEAVE MY SON ERIX ON DEPOSIT TO BUY THIS SHIP!

NEXT INSTALMENT COMING UP, SIR! EGYPTIAN SHIP TO STARBOARD.

SPLENDID! WE'LL MAKE OUR FORTUNES! WE'LL DO IT YET! GET READY TO BOARD HER!

113

114

AS SOON AS WE LAND I'LL TAKE YOU TO THE PALACE TO MEET THE QUEEN.

AND IN HER PALACE THE LUXURY-LOVING CLEOPATRA IS SITTING DOWN TO HER FAVOURITE SNACK – PEARLS DISSOLVED IN VINEGAR.

WHERE ARE THE PEARL TONGS, FOR OSIRIS'S SAKE?

HERE, TASTER! GET ON WITH YOUR JOB!

VERY WELL, O QUEEN!

THE GREEDY PIG! SHE'S TAKEN FOUR PEARLS AGAIN!

UGH! I DO HATE TOO MUCH PEARL IN MY VINEGAR!

EDIFIS THE ARCHITECT CRAVES THE HONOUR OF AN AUDIENCE!

SHOW HIM IN...

MEET MY FRIENDS FROM GAUL, O QUEEN – A POWERFUL MAGICIAN AND TWO BRAVE WARRIORS WHO HAVE COME TO HELP ME...

DOGMATIX!

GRRROARRR!

VERY WELL, BUT GET ON WITH IT! THERE ISN'T MUCH TIME LEFT, AND CAESAR KEEPS NEEDLING ME. IF YOU SUCCEED THERE'LL BE GOLD ALL ROUND. IF NOT – THE CROCODILES!

AND I WARN YOU, EDIFIS, YOUR RIVAL ARTIFIS IS NOT PLEASED THAT I CHOSE YOU AND NOT HIM TO BUILD CAESAR'S PALACE. HE'D LOVE TO SEE YOU END UP INSIDE A CROCODILE. YOU MAY GO.

SHE LOOKS BAD TEMPERED, BUT SHE HAS A PRETTY NOSE...

VERY PRETTY!

115

COME HOME TO MY HOUSE...

IS THIS IT?

ER... YES. YES, I DESIGNED IT MYSELF.

EDIFIS

THE DOOR'S JAMMED AGAIN... I MUST HAVE MADE A MISTAKE IN MY PLANS SOMEWHERE.

I'LL GIVE YOU A HAND.

CRASH!

OBELIX, NO!

NO, REALLY, IT'S QUITE ALL RIGHT! IT'S MORE USE THIS WAY!

ER... WATCH OUT FOR THE STEPS!

I GET THE IMPRESSION YOU REALLY DID NEED OUR HELP, EDIFIS.

THIS IS WHERE I WORK... MEET MY FAITHFUL SCRIBE EXLIBRIS. HE SPEAKS YOUR LANGUAGE FLUENTLY. HE SPEAKS ALL MODERN LANGUAGES – LATIN, GREEK, CELTIC, ETC...

IS IT A GOOD POSITION BEING A SCRIBE?

OH, IT'S VERY COMFORTABLE! I'M SITTING PRETTY – SQUATTING, RATHER!

HOW DOES ONE BECOME A SCRIBE?

I TOOK A CORRESPONDENCE COURSE... A VERY GOOD COLLEGE...

THE ADVERTISEMENT SAID, ANYONE WHO COULD DRAW COULD WRITE!

118

DURING THE LENTIL* BREAK THE LABOURERS HAVE AN UNEXPECTED VISITOR...

* A VERY POPULAR ANCIENT EGYPTIAN DISH

?! !?!
?! ?!?
? ?!
?

...WHOSE REMARKS ARE EVIDENTLY OF ABSORBING INTEREST.

TEEHEEHEE!

AND AT THE END OF THE LENTIL BREAK...

BOUHOUHOUHO

...THE LABOURERS MAKE IT PERFECTLY CLEAR...

...THAT THEY ARE NOT GOING BACK TO WORK.

MASTER! THE LABOURERS WON'T GO ON WITH THE JOB! I THINK SOMEONE'S BEEN STIRRING THEM UP AGAINST YOU!

?

ALL THESE WORRIES ARE POSITIVELY BLOOD-CURDLING! BY THE TIME THE CROCODILES GET ME I'LL BE QUITE UNEATABLE!

ALL THE BETTER! ARE YOU SO KEEN TO MAKE THEM A GOOD MEAL?

BUT THOSE ARE SACRED CROCODILES! YOU CAN'T JUST FEED THEM ANY OLD THING!

THESE EGYPTIANS ARE CRAZY!

TAP! TAP! TAP!

119

120

121

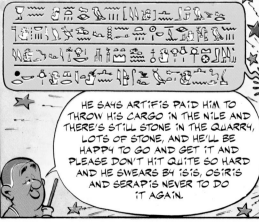

123

125

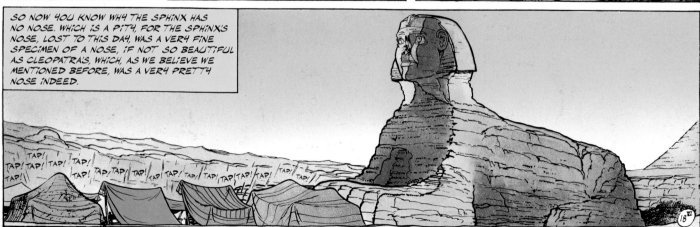

So now you know why the Sphinx has no nose. Which is a pity, for the Sphinx's nose, lost to this day, was a very fine specimen of a nose, if not so beautiful as Cleopatra's, which, as we believe we mentioned before, was a very pretty nose indeed.

INSIDE THE PYRAMID...

MY POWERS ARE NOT STRONG ENOUGH TO GET US OUT OF HERE... I AM VERY MUCH AFRAID THIS MAY BE THE END OF OUR ADVENTURES, BY BELENOS!

I'M ONLY SORRY FOR EDIFIS... WITHOUT OUR HELP HE'LL END UP INSIDE A CROCODILE.

WELL, I'M SORRY FOR MY POOR LITTLE DOGMATIX... AREN'T I, DOGMATIX?

DOGMATIX?!

YES, DOGMATIX! WHAT ABOUT IT? YOU'RE NOT GOING TO BE CROSS WITH ME FOR BRINGING HIM? ANYWAY, I DIDN'T BRING HIM, HE CAME ALL BY HIMSELF!

EXACTLY! HE'S FOUND US THANKS TO HIS NOSE... IN WHICH CASE HE CAN FIND HIS WAY BACK AGAIN AND SHOW US THE WAY OUT!

BY BELENOS, YOU'RE RIGHT!

DOGMATIX, IF YOU HELP US OUT OF HERE YOU'LL GET A VERY BIG BONE OUTSIDE!

YOU'LL GET TWO BIG BONES!

HEAPS OF BIG BONES!

OBELIX, I APOLOGIZE! YOU WERE QUITE RIGHT TO BRING YOUR DOGGIE!

SOMETIMES I FEEL HE UNDERSTANDS EVERYTHING I SAY!

129

1 THE FOREIGNERS HAVE DISAPPEARED, THERE'S NO NEED FOR YOU TO GO ON WITH YOUR JOURNEY.
2 I GOT IT FIRST TIME.

IT'S MAGIC! YOU'RE WIZARDS! ONLY A SUPERMAN COULD EVER FIND HIS WAY OUT OF...

WHAM!

THE BOATS SET OFF AGAIN AND SAIL PEACEFULLY ON UP THE NILE...

SCRUNCH! SCRUNCH! SCRUNCH!

...STOPPING OFF TO SEE THE SIGHTS AT INTERESTING SPOTS SUCH AS LUXOR...

NO, NO, AND FOR THE THIRD TIME NO, OBELIX! THAT THING IN THE MIDDLE OF THE VILLAGE? IT WOULD JUST LOOK SILLY.

WE SHALL NEVER BE IN CONCORD OVER THIS!

MEANWHILE, BACK AT ALEXANDRIA...

O ARTIFIS, MY MASTER... THEY'RE WIZARDS! THEY HAVE SUPERHUMAN POWERS!

!?

THEY'VE MANAGED TO GET OUT OF THE LABYRINTH OF THE GREAT PYRAMID!

FANTASTIC! THEY'RE JUST FANTASTIC!

ALL THE MORE REASON TO FIND SOME WAY OF STOPPING THEM! EDIFIS MUST NOT BUILD THAT PALACE, KRUKHUT!

131

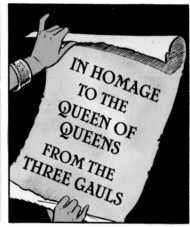

132

138

ARE YOU ALL RIGHT, EDIFIS?

NOT BAD... A LITTLE DIZZY!

POOR OLD EDIFIS, IT MUST BE ON ACCOUNT OF HIS SUFFERINGS!

I GIVE IN! I HOPED TO STOP YOU FINISHING THE PALACE. NO HARD FEELINGS?

NO HARD FEELINGS, AND TO PROVE IT WE'LL TAKE YOU TWO ALONG WITH US. WE'VE GOT A JOB FOR YOU.

SOON AFTERWARDS, AT THE BUILDING SITE...

THIS IS WHAT COMES OF ALL THOSE WICKED THINGS YOU MADE ME DO, BOSS!

SHUT UP AND PULL, WILL YOU!

THE BUILDING'S COMING ALONG NICELY, EDIFIS.

THANKS TO YOU THREE, GETAFIX!

MEANWHILE, IN CLEOPATRA'S PALACE...

AVE, CLEOPATRA. WELL, HOW'S THE PALACE GOING? TIME WILL SOON BE UP.

AVE, CAESAR. OH, IT'S GETTING ON NICELY, THANKS, JULIUS! WE'LL SOON BE ABLE TO HAVE A LITTLE PALACE WARMING.

AVE, CAESAR!

AVE! LEGIONARY, GO AND FIND MINTJULEP MY EGYPTIAN SPY.

AVE, CAESAR!

AVE, AVE, MINTJULEP. I LOOK LIKE LOSING FACE WITH CLEOPATRA...

I WAS TOLD THAT EDIFIS THE ARCHITECT WAS A NITWIT, BUT NOW IT SEEMS THE PALACE WILL BE READY IN TIME. GO TO THE BUILDING SITE AND SEE WHAT'S GOING ON, BY JUPITER!

140

141

* ANCIENT GAULISH WAR-SONG

142

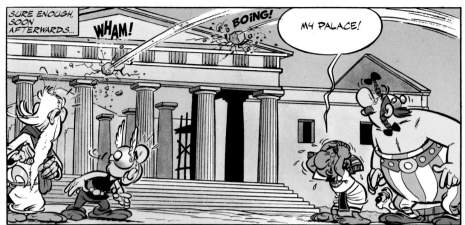

145

WATCH OUT! ONE OF THE BESIEGED MEN IS TRYING TO BREAK IN AGAIN!

WHOOSH!

HERE YOU ARE, OBELIX! DOGMATIX HAS JUST GOT BACK! HE DID HIS JOB PERFECTLY!

THERE YOU ARE! YOU SEE?

LET'S HOPE THE QUEEN ACTS QUICKLY. THE ROMAN MISSILES ARE DESTROYING THE PALACE!

SURE ENOUGH, IN THE CAMP OF THE BESIEGING ARMY...

THERE YOU ARE, CAESAR! EVEN IF WE DON'T CAPTURE THEM THE PALACE WILL BE DESTROYED JUST THE SAME!

EXCELLENT, OPERACHORUS, EXCELLENT!

AVE, CAESAR... ER... SOMEONE WANTS TO SPEAK TO YOU...

WHO IS IT?

ZING! BOOM!

TAPTAPTAP! TAPTAP TAP!

TANTANTARA!!!

?!?

*A RARE OCCURRENCE IN THE BUILDING TRADE AT THAT TIME.

150

151

AFTER A LUXURY CRUISE LASTING SEVERAL WEEKS...

SCRUNCH!

SCRUNCH!

...THEY AT LAST SIGHT...

A SAIL! A SAIL! ASTERIX, OBELIX AND GETAFIX ARE BACK!

THE GAULISH VILLAGE WELCOMES HOME ITS HEROES WITH ITS USUAL ENTHUSIASM AND FEASTING...

...AND IT WAS ALL THANKS TO DOGMATIX!

A NOSE, MY DEAR FELLOW, WHAT A NOSE!

I WILL NOW COMPOSE A LITTLE SONG...

AND FOR THE NEXT FEW DAYS, EVERYONE IS HAPPY.... AT LEAST, NEARLY EVERYONE...

NO, OBELIX, NO!

I DON'T LIKE THE DESIGN OF YOUR NEW MENHIRS! LET'S KEEP IT GAULISH!

THE END

UDERZO